For Mum.

You might be small on the outside, but I've never known

anyone with such a BIG heart on the inside.

I don't know what I'd do without you.

Love you to the stars and beyond xxx

- L.E.A.

BLOOMSBURY CHILDREN'S BOOKS
Bloomsbury Publishing Plc
50 Bedford Square, London, WC1B 3DP, UK

BLOOMSBURY, BLOOMSBURY CHILDREN'S BOOKS and the Diana logo are
trademarks of Bloomsbury Publishing Plc

First published in Great Britain 2019 by Bloomsbury Publishing Plc

Text and illustrations copyright © Laura Ellen Anderson 2019

Laura Ellen Anderson has asserted her rights under the Copyright,
Designs and Patents Act, 1988, to be identified as the Author and Illustrator of this work

A catalogue record for this book is available from the British Library

ISBN: HB: 978 1 4088 9407 1
PB: 978 1 4088 9406 4
eBook: 978 1 4088 9408 8

2 4 6 8 10 9 7 5 3 1

Printed and bound in China by Leo

All papers used by Bloomsbury Publishing Plc are natural, recyclable products
from wood grown in well managed forests. The manufacturing
processes conform to the environmental regulations of the country of origin

To find out more about our authors and books visit www.bloomsbury.com and sign up for our newsletters

LAURA ELLEN ANDERSON

I DON'T WANT TO BE SMALL

BLOOMSBURY
CHILDREN'S BOOKS
LONDON OXFORD NEW YORK NEW DELHI SYDNEY

NO!

It's NOT FAIR.
I don't want
to be

small.

I want to grow FASTER
so I can be tall!

I'm always on tiptoes. In crowds I can't see!
And ALL of my friends are MUCH taller than me.

It appears I'm SO small they forget that I'm there . . .

THE
BEST-MOST-MEGA
ROLLER-COASTER

YOU MUST BE THIS
BIG
TO RIDE

and I can't even go on
BIG rides at the fair.

My brother is lucky
for being so TALL.
He gives me his clothes
when he finds them too small.

But his clothes
are too BIG,
it's just SO unfair!

I'm so MAD, I throw Teddy Bear up in the air.

OOPS!

Now he's stuck!
Oh, what have I done?
Being this small ruins
all of my fun!

I try jumping
to reach him,

I stand on
a box.

I try stilts

and a long stick –

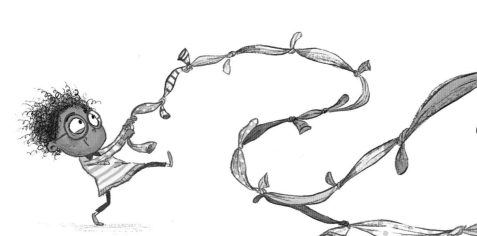

a rope made
of socks.

Perhaps if I eat all my greens REALLY FAST,
I'll grow super quick and save Teddy at last!

But, NO, I'm just full with strange sounds in my belly . . .
I'm STILL the same height, but . . . NOW SO MUCH MORE SMELLY!

Maybe I'll grow if
I'm more like a flower,

so I sit in the sunshine

and have the odd shower.

But now I'm just **wet**,
and there's **mud**
in my hair.

I will **never** be tall, and . . .

"Nice bear!" says a girl
who's much taller than me.
"Would you like me to help
get it down from that tree?"

The girl reaches up . . .
But it's still far too **high**.
"Oh dear, what a pickle,"
I slump down and sigh.

But just when I think that my bear's **stuck** forever,

I gasp and say, "We could reach Teddy **together!**"

The next thing I know
I'm the **tallest** around!
I've never been SO far
away from the ground!

We laugh and

we **wobble,**

and then

one,

two,

three...

Together we finally
set my bear free!

"Thank you!" I say,
and I hold out my bear.
"Here, this is Teddy,
perhaps we can share?"

So, yes I am small,
but now I don't mind,

I've made a new friend
and she's mightily kind!

We play games and laugh
for the rest of the day –

I'm small and  she's tall and . . .

we're
PERFECT
that way!